This book belongs to:

....

Retold by Gaby Goldsack

Illustrated by Ruth Galloway

Language consultants: Betty Root and Monica Hughes

This edition published by Parragon in 2009

Parragon
Queen Street House
4 Queen Street
Bath BA1 1HE, UK

ISBN 978-1-4054-8709-2
Printed in China

Snow White
and the
Seven Dwarfs

PaRragon

Bath · New York · Singapore · Hong Kong · Cologne · Delhi · Melbourne

Notes for Parents

These **Gold Stars**® reading books encourage and support children who are learning to read.

Starting to read

• Start by reading the book aloud to your child. Take time to talk about the pictures. They often give clues about the story. The easy-to-read speech bubbles provide an excellent 'joining-in' activity.

• Over time, try to read the same book several times. Gradually your child will want to read the book aloud with you. It helps to run your finger under the words as you say them.

• Occasionally, stop and encourage your child to continue reading aloud without you. Join in again when your

child needs help. This is the next step towards helping your child become an independent reader.

• Finally, your child will be ready to read alone. Listen carefully and give plenty of praise. Remember to make reading an enjoyable experience.

Using your stickers

The fun colour stickers in the centre of the book and

fold-out scene board at the back will help your child re-enact parts of the story, again and again.

Remember these four stages:

• Read the story **to** your child.

• Read the story **with** your child.

• Encourage your child to read **to you**.

• Listen to your child read **alone**.

Once upon a time there was a king and a queen.
They had a beautiful baby girl.

The king and queen called her Snow White.

The queen died soon after Snow White
was born.

The king was sad and lonely.

But, one year later, the king married again.

The new queen was very beautiful.

She liked to look at herself in a mirror.

The queen had one special mirror. It was magic. Everyday she looked into the magic mirror and said,

"Mirror, mirror on the wall, who is the fairest of them all?"

And the mirror would answer,

"You are the fairest."

12

One day the queen looked into the mirror
and said,

"Mirror, mirror on the wall,
who is the fairest of them all?"

And the mirror said,

"You were the fairest, shining bright.
But now the fairest is Snow White."

The queen was very cross.
She called for a servant.

"Take Snow White into the
forest and kill her,"
said the queen.

I don't want
to kill you.

The servant took Snow White into the forest.

"I don't want to kill you. Run away please," he said. And he walked away.

"Please don't leave me," said Snow White. He left her near a cottage.

Snow White walked to the cottage.

She knocked at the door. There was no answer so she went in.

She saw seven little chairs around a little table. Then she saw seven little beds.

Snow White was very tired. She lay down on one of the beds.

Seven little dwarfs lived in the cottage. Each day they went into the hills to dig for gold.

That night they came back to the cottage.

They found Snow White fast asleep.

When she woke up she told them her story.

"You can stay with us," said the dwarfs.

The queen was very cross. She put some poison in an apple. She dressed up as an old woman and went to the cottage.

Snow White opened the door and saw the old woman.

"Would you like an apple?" the old woman asked.

"Yes please," said Snow White. She took one bite and fell to the ground.

When the seven dwarfs came home, they could not wake Snow White. They were very sad.

The dwarfs put Snow White in a glass box.

A prince came riding by. He saw Snow White.

"What a beautiful girl," he said.

The prince opened the glass box.
He kissed Snow White.

The kiss woke her up. She saw the prince
and fell in love with him.

"Will you marry me?" asked the prince.

"Yes!" said Snow White.

One day the queen
looked in her magic
mirror and the
mirror said,

"You were the fairest,
shining bright.
But now much fairer is
Snow White."

The queen was so cross
that she disappeared.

Snow White and the prince married and
lived happily ever after.

Read and Say

How many of these words can you say?
The pictures will help you. Look back in
your book and see if you can find the
words in the story.

apple

king

Snow White

queen

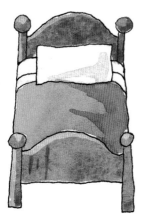

bed

prince

mirror

forest

dwarfs

cottage

29